To my daddy
love from

Florence xxxxD

Why I Love My Daddy

Illustrated by Daniel Howarth

HarperCollins *Children's Books*

I love my daddy because...

he is big and strong.

I love my daddy because...

he is clever.

I love my daddy because...

he keeps me safe and cosy.

I love my daddy because...

he plays with me.

I love my daddy because...

he carries me.

I love my daddy because...

he is handsome.

I love my daddy because...

he is funny.

I love my daddy because...

he hugs me good night.

I love my daddy because...

he fixes things.

I love my daddy because...

he tickles me.

I love my daddy because...

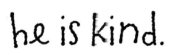

he is kind.

I love my daddy because...

he has the best ideas.

I love my daddy because...

he is my best friend.

Everyone loves
their daddy —

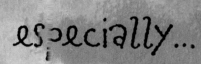

especially...

ME!